First published 2016 by Nosy Crow Ltd
The Crow's Nest, 14 Baden Place, Crosby Row
London SE1 1YW
www.nosycrow.com

This edition published 2019

ISBN 978 1 78800 373 5

Nosy Crow and associated logos are trademarks
and /or registered trademarks of Nosy Crow Ltd.

Text and illustration © Elys Dolan 2016
The right of Elys Dolan to be identified as the
author and illustrator of this work has
been asserted.

A CIP catalogue record for this book is available
from the British Library.

Papers used by Nosy Crow are made from
wood grown in sustainable forests.
Printed in China

THE DOUGHNUT of DOOM

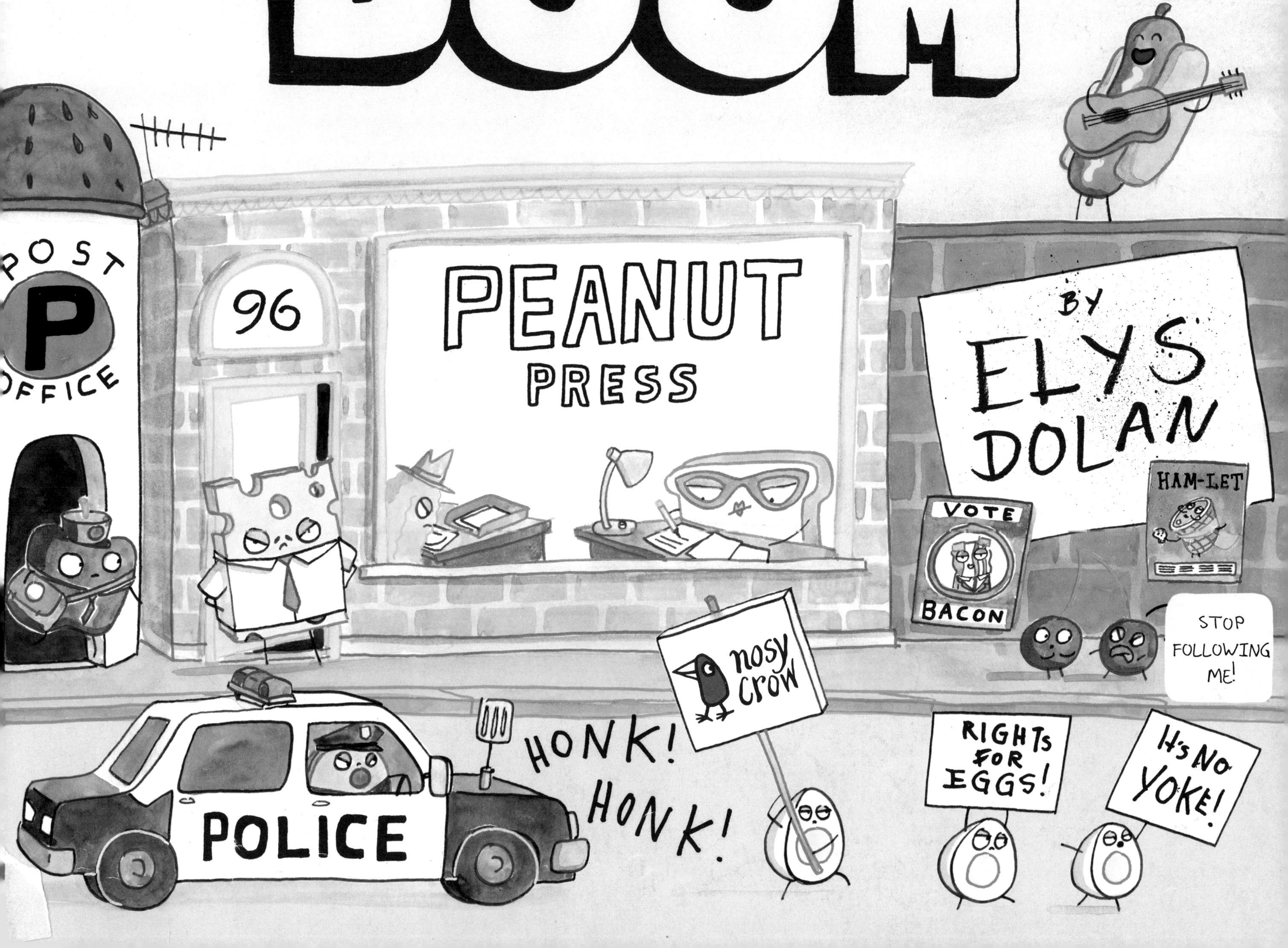

My name's Nancy McNutty, trainee reporter. I was just a peanut butter sandwich trying to get my big break in a tough world.

But it wasn't proving easy.
Especially with a boss like Big Cheese.

But then the phone rang. It was Marvin, my sauce at Lemon Labs.

The situation sounded serious so I knew I had to get to Lemon Labs – FAST!

I needed to catch up with the monster but there was already panic amongst the citizens. So, I hitched a lift through the crowd.

The fire service tried to control it.

Citizens, remain calm! I can confirm that there
is a giant doughnut destroying the city. The proper
authorities are dealing with it as we speak.
Stay in your homes and try not to look tasty...
who am I kidding? It's unstoppable! We're out of options!
Evacuate the city! PANIC!

I'd seen enough destruction and knew this had to stop. But how?
I was just a peanut butter sandwich – what could I do?
It was time to talk to Professor Nutcase.

That's when I knew it was time to stop reporting the action and be a part of it.

And then . . . everything went black.

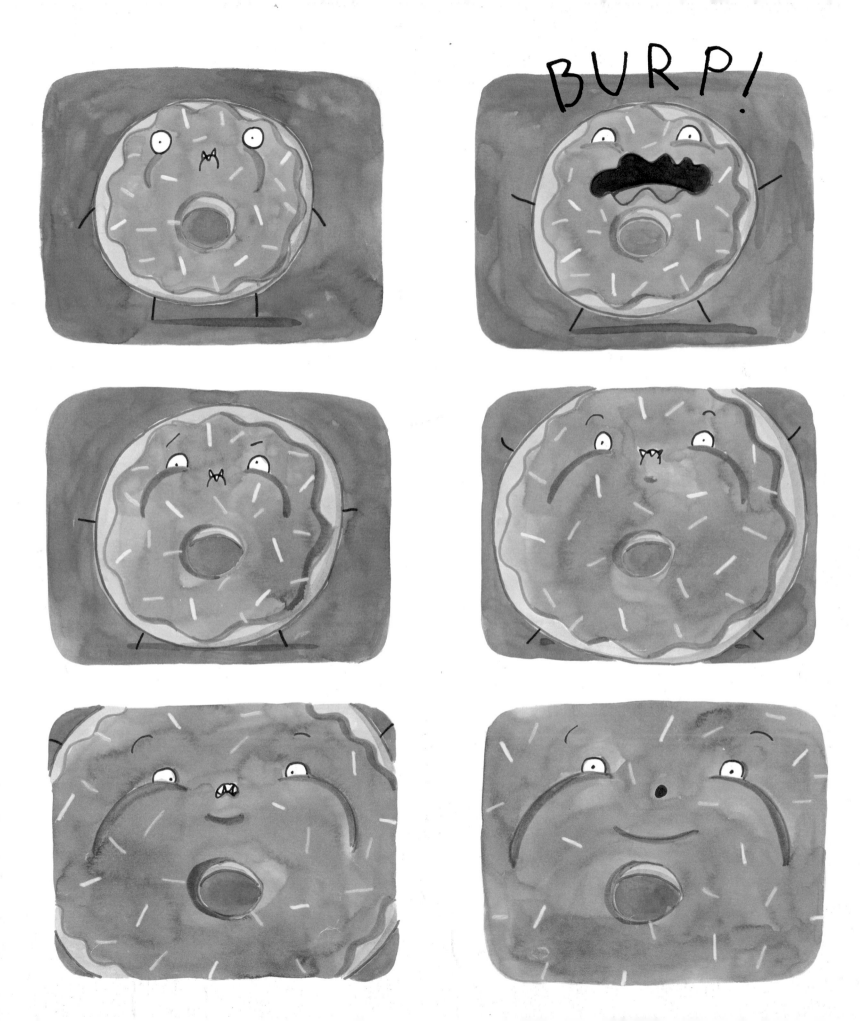

That day, instead of writing the news, I **was** the news.

And once again, Food Town was safe.